Fire Slinger

Fire Slinger

Despair

Josh Zimmer

Superstar Speedsters

The book has been inspired by other superhero franchises such as My Hero Academia, Marvel, DC, and Power Rangers!

CONTENTS

book

In the villain hideout, Ben shot an ice blast at the book shelf, and froze it in a sheet of ice. Norman and Otto were amazed by their creation. Ben summoned an wall of ice, and froze Otto and Norman on to the wall. Ben backflipped on to the desk, as Norman ignited an blast of energy from his body. The ice wall shattered, as Otto and Norman landed on the ground. Ben backflipped off of the desk, and smashed the window open with a ice beam. Ben jumped out of the window, and skated on a sheet of ice toward Justin's house. Justin was at Oasis Falls High School, cleaning up the mess from Norman's rampage. Justin straightened the desks in their rows, and reorganized the teacher's desk in the study hall. Down the street, Ben was skating on the sheet of ice, causing chaos in Zoompolis. Ben walked in to the gas station, and walked toward the cash register. The cashier's name was Daniel. Daniel said, "How can I help you?" Ben's eyes glowed blue, as he summoned a icicle in to his hand. Ben walked toward Daniel, and kicked him in the chest. Daniel bent down, and grabbed his chest. Daniel growled, and threw an punch at Ben. Ben grabbed Daniel's arm, and broke it. Daniel screamed in pain, as he slid backwards. Ben sped in to Daniel! Ben grabbed Daniel by the neck, and threw him in to the wall. Daniel laid next to the wall. Ben wrapped his arm around Daniel's neck, and stabbed the icicle in to Daniel's head. Blood poured on to the ground, as Daniel laid on the ground. Ben ignited a ice blast from his body. The ice blast covered the area, as the gas station exploded. Glass shards and broken items covered the area, as Ben walked through the debris. Police cars sped toward the debris, and stopped next to it. The police officers walked out of their cars, and cleaned up the debris from the area. Ben summoned a sheet of ice, and skated further down the street. Cars were speeding past Ben on the street, as he was skating on the sheet of ice. Ben skated to Justin's house, as the birds tweeted in the background. Ben saw Justin's house, and backflipped off of the sheet of ice. Ben landed on the ground and walked through the grass toward Justin's house. As Ben walked through the grass, the ground turned in to ice. Spider Crusader walked out of the house, and saw Ben. Spider Crusader growled, as he walked toward Ben. Spider Crusader swung through the air, and shot a web at Ben's chest. The web attached to Ben's chest, as Spider Crusader slingshot himself toward Ben. Ben summoned an ice shield, and hit Spider Crusader in the chest. Spider Crusader smashed in to the house. The house shook, as Spider Crusader regained his balance. Ben's eyes glowed blue, as he threw an ice ball at Spider Crusader. Spider Crusader dodged the ice ball. Spider Crusader backflipped, and shot webs at Ben. Ben threw ice balls at the webs, and turned them in to ice. Ben used his powers to throw the ice webs at Spider Crusader. Spider Crusader backflipped out of the way. The ice webs hit the tree. The tree froze in a sheet of ice. Spider Crusader landed on the ground. Spider Crusader backflipped, and kicked Ben in the face. Ben froze his head in a sheet of ice. Spider Crusader's leg froze up in a sheet of ice. Ben ignited an ice blast from his body. Spider Crusader smashed in to the tree. Spider Crusader laid against the tree, as he rubbed his head. Ben sped in to the tree! Spider Crusader's senses tingled, and he backflipped over Ben. Spider Crusader kicked Ben in the back. Ben slid backwards, and threw a ice ball at Spider Crusader. Spider Crusader made a baseball bat with his webs, and hit the ice ball back at Ben. Ben summoned a icicle, and sliced the ice ball in half. Ben shot multiple ice blasts at Spider Crusader. Spider Crusader backflipped, and dodged the ice blasts. Spider Crusader flipped in the air, and landed behind Ben. Ben spun in a circle, and kicked Spider Crusader in the chest. Spider Crusader slid backwards! Spider Crusader threw a punch at Ben's face. Ben caught Spider Crusader's arm, and kicked him in the face. Spider Crusader rolled on the ground. Spider Crusader got up from the ground. Ben sped in to Spider Crusader, and punched him in the face. Spider Crusader fell on to the ground! Ben held Spider Crusader on the ground! Ben punched Spider Crusader in the face, multiple times. Blood dripped from Spider Crusader's armor. Spider Crusader shot a web at Ben's face. Ben froze his face with a sheet of ice, and the web froze in to a ice cube, and smashed on the ground. Ben picked up Spider Crusader by his neck, and threw him in to the tree. Spider Crusader smashed through the tree, and rolled on the ground. Spider Crusader backflipped off of the ground. Ben shot ice blasts at Spider Crusader. Spider Crusader dodged the ice blasts. Spider Crusader shot a web at Ben's chest. Spider Crusader pulled on the web, and dragged Ben closer to him. Spider Crusader kicked Ben in the chest. Ben smashed in to the wall, and laid next to it. Spider Crusader sped toward Ben. Ben backflipped out of the way, and threw a ice blast at Spider Crusader. The ice blast hit Spider Crusader in the chest. Spider Crusader slid in to a tree. Ben tackled Spider Crusader through the tree, and smashed him in to the ground. Ben froze his arm in to a sheet of ice, as he punched Spider Crusader in the face, multiple times. Spider Crusader's helmet started to crack, as he growled. Ben continued punching Spider Crusader in the face. Spider Crusader's helmet shattered, as blood poured on to the ground. Ben grabbed Spider Crusader by the neck, and picked him up from the ground. Spider Crusader struggled in Ben's grip. Ben smashed Spider Crusader against the wall, multiple times. Spider Crusader's armor started to crack. Ben held Spider Crusader on the wall, as he punched him in the face, multiple times. Spider Crusader growled, as blood dripped on to the ground, from his face. Spider Crusader held his arm up, and pressed a button on his wrist. Spider Crusader's communicator activated, as Spider Crusader started talking in to it. Spider Crusader said, "Justin, come in! I need help!" Further down the street, Justin was in the middle of cleaning up the debris at Oasis Falls High School. Justin lifted his arm up, and pressed the button on his wrist. Justin's communicator activated, as Justin started talking in to it. Justin said, "Hey Spider Crusader, what's up!" Spider Crusader spoke in to the communicator and said, "There's a supervillain, and I am having trouble defending myself!" Justin spoke in to the communicator and said, "I am on my way!" Spider Crusader spoke in to the communicator and said, 'Please hurry!" Justin climbed out of the window, and summoned a sheet of flames. Justin skated on the sheet of flames toward his house. Ben grabbed Spider Crusader's arm, and destroyed Spider Crusader's communicator, with a ice blast. Spider Crusader screamed in pain. Ben tightened his grip on Spider Crusader's neck, as he smashed Spider Crusader in to the ground, multiple times. Spider Crusader's armor shattered, as he screamed in pain. Blood poured on to the ground, from Spider Crusader's body. Ben lifted Spider Crusader in to the air, and threw him in to the tree. Spider Crusader smashed in to the tree, and rolled on the ground. Spider Crusader laid on the ground. Ben jumped on to Spider Crusader, and punched him in the face. Blood poured from Spider Crusader's face, as he laid on the ground. Ben grabbed Spider Crusader by the neck, and lifted him in to the air. Ben squeezed Spider Crusader's neck, and choked him. Spider Crusader coughed, as he struggled in Ben's grip. Ben smashed Spider Crusader in to the wall. The wall crumbled, as Spider Crusader laid on the ground. Ben held Spider Crusader on the ground, and punched him in the face. Blood poured on the ground! Ben shot a ice blast at Spider Crusader. The ice blast smashed Spider Crusader through the ground, leaving a hollowed dent. Spider Crusader laid on the ground, with a puddle of blood under him. Justin reached his house, and backflipped off of the sheet of flames. Justin landed in front of Ben. Ben growled, while his eyes glowed blue. Spider Crusader slowly got up from the ground, and smiled at the sight of Justin. Spider Crusader stabbed a health pack in to his arm. Spider Crusader crawled behind the bush, and cleaned the blood off of him with a towel. Justin's eyes glowed red, as he walked toward Ben. Justin shot a fire blast at Ben. The fire blast smashed Ben in to the tree. Ben laid next to the tree. Justin backflipped, and hit Ben in the face with a roundhouse kick. Ben slid backwards, and smashed through the tree. Ben punched Justin in the face. Justin dodged Ben's arm, and punched Ben in the chest. Ben slid backwards, and shot a ice blast at Justin. Justin dodged the ice blast, and threw a fire ball at Ben. Ben got hit by the fire ball, and smashed in to the house. The house shook, as Ben laid next to it. Ben regained his balance, and flipped on to the tree. Ben swung on the tree branch. Ben swung off of the tree branch, and landed on the ground. Justin threw an fire ball at Ben. Ben dodged the fire ball. The fire ball bounced off of the pole, and hit the wall. Ben threw an ice ball at Justin! Justin dodged the ice ball, and the ice ball hit an car speeding through the street. The car froze in a block of ice, and smashed in to the pole. Ben growled, and sped toward Justin. Ben swung his leg at Justin's face. Justin dodged Ben's leg, and grabbed it with his hand. Justin lit Ben's leg on fire. Ben screamed in pain, as he rolled on the ground. Ben froze his leg in ice to cool himself down. Ben backflipped off of the ground. Justin sped in to Ben! Justin grabbed Ben by the neck, and smashed him in to the ground. Justin punched Ben in the face, multiple times. Blood poured on the ground from Ben's face. Ben growled, as he grabbed Justin's arm. Justin lit his arm on fire. Ben screamed in pain, as his arm got barbecued. Justin growled, as he picked up Ben's body, and threw him in to the wall. Ben smashed through the wall, as blood dripped on the ground from his body. Ben got up from the ground, and growled. Ben ignited an ice blast from his body. The ice blast covered the area, and made the house explode. Aaron and Sunshine laid on the ground, as they coughed. Ben threw an ice whip at Aaron and Sunshine. The ice whip wrapped around Aaron and Sunshine's body. Ben pulled on the ice whip, and dragged Aaron and Sunshine closer to him. Ben summoned an ice sword in to his hand! Ben swung the ice sword at Aaron and Sunshine! The ice sword sliced the bodies of Aaron and Sunshine in half, and killed them. Aaron and Sunshine's bodies laid on the ground, in puddles of blood. Ben laughed maniacally, as he threw an ice blast at Justin. Justin threw an fire blast at Ben. The fire blast and the ice blast collided with each other, and caused a huge blast in the area. The huge blast destroyed all of the trees in the area. Justin's eyes turned flaming red, as he growled in anger. Justin summoned an aura of flames around his body, and shot a flaming blast at Ben from his arm. The flaming blast hit Ben in the chest, and smashed him through the ground. Ben laid on the ground, with blood pouring from his body. Justin growled, as he walked closer to Ben. Justin jumped on to Ben, and punched him in the face, multiple times. Blood dripped from Ben's face! Ben's eyes glowed blue, as he ignited a ice blast from his body. Justin slid backwards, and rolled on the ground! Justin backflipped off of the ground. Ben backflipped off of the ground! Ben threw ice balls at Justin. Justin dodged the ice balls. Ben ignited an icy aura around his body, and sped in to Justin. Ben tackled Justin in to the wall. Justin laid next to the wall, as he growled. Ben growled, as he punched Justin in the face, multiple times. The flames from Justin's body protected Justin from the punches. Ben growled, as he continued trying to punch Justin in the face. The flames from Justin's body absorbed the punches, and burnt Ben's arm. Justin growled, and kicked Ben in the chest. Ben slid backwards! Justin ignited an fire blast from his body. Ben rolled on the ground. Ben backflipped off of the ground. Justin sped in to Ben, and smashed him in to the tree. The tree fell on to the ground. Justin grabbed Ben by his neck, and lifted him in to the air. Justin crushed Ben's neck, and smashed him in to the ground. Ben coughed, as he laid on the ground. Justin punched Ben in the face, multiple times. Blood dripped from Ben's face, as Justin continued punching him. The puddle of blood grew, as blood poured from Ben's face. Justin growled, as he lit up his arm with flames. Justin put his hand on Ben's chest, and burnt his body in to a crisp. Ben's body turned in to ash on the ground. The ash blew away in a gust of wind. Justin's eyes turned back to normal, as the aura of flames disappeared around him. Justin wiped the blood off of his body with a towel. Justin walked to the bush, and sat next to Spider Crusader. Spider Crusader and Justin hugged each other. The clean up crew drove up the street, and parked next to the debris. The clean up crew cleared the debris from the area. Spider Crusader repaired the web shooters on his arm. Justin laid next to the bush, and looked at the clouds. Down the street, the villains were frustrated at the villain hideout. Norman growled, and pushed Otto in to the wall. Norman said, "Heroes are pests, they like to ruin our fun. Otto said, "I wish there was a way to stop the heroes from destroying our experiments." Norman smiled, as he thought of a perfect plan to deal with the heroes. Norman said, "We need to slow the heroes down, which means that we need to work harder to make our experiments better, and stronger." Otto smiled and said, "You always think of the best plans!" Back at the bush, Justin got up from the ground. Justin summoned a sheet of flames, and skated to Oasis Falls High School. Spider Crusader flipped in to the air, and web sung in the air. Spider Crusader followed Justin to Oasis Falls High School. Justin and Spider Crusader got to Oasis Falls High School, and walked in to the courtyard. Justin and Spider Crusader walked through the courtyard, and walked to the doors. Justin and Spider Crusader walked through the doors of Oasis Falls High School. The other students were walking toward the gym. Spider Crusader and Justin followed the other students in to the gym. Justin and Spider Crusader walked toward the bleachers. Justin and Spider Crusader walked up the bleachers. Justin and Spider Crusader sat on the bleachers. The other students sat on the bleachers. The mascot for Oasis Falls High School backflipped in to the gym, and did some flips in the air. The cheerleaders cheered, while the marching band marched in to the gym. The basketball players walked in to the middle of the gym. The basketball players got in to position, as the coach played some music through the school speakers. Drew dribbled the basketball and sung, "We are the Oasis Falls Wildcats!" Drew passed the basketball to Sam! Sam sung while dribbling the basketball, "We are the best team in the world!" Sam passed the basketball to David. David threw the basketball in to the net and sung "We Can crush our opponents, because we are the Amazing Wildcats!" The basketball went in to the net, and bounced on the ground. The students cheered, as the mascot flipped in the air. The cheerleaders flipped in to the air and said, "Lets Go Wildcats!" The basketball players went in to the middle of the gym, and dribbled the ball to each other. Drew spun the basketball on his finger, as the the students cheered. The cheerleaders shook their pom poms, and the mascot flipped in the air. The music stopped playing on the school speakers. The marching band played their instruments for an hour, while the mascot did some flips in the air. The school bell rang in the background. The marching band walked out of the gym, and in to the teacher's lounge. The mascot and the cheerleaders walked out of the gym, and in to the teacher's lounge. The other students walked out of the gym. Justin and Spider Crusader walked out of the gym. Justin and Spider Crusader walked in to the hallway. Justin and Spider Crusader walked out of the hallway, and in to the courtyard for Oasis Falls High School. Justin and Spider Crusader sat on the stairs for Oasis Falls High School. The wind was blowing through Justin's hair, and the birds were tweeting in the background. The bugs were buzzing and the dogs were chasing the squirrels down the street. The sun was setting, and the sun set was amazing. An pack of wolves walked in to the courtyard, and were antagonizing a group of squirrels. The wolves walked closer to the squirrels. The squirrels backed up in to the tree, and they were terrified in fear. The wolves growled, and charged at the squirrels. The wolves pounced on the squirrels! The wolves picked up the squirrels with their fangs, and bit down on the squirrel's fur. Blood poured on the ground from the body of the squirrels. The wolves spit out the squirrels, and they laid on the ground, in puddles of blood. The wolves growled, and walked closer to Spider Crusader. Spider Crusader shot a web at the wolves. The web attached the wolves to the tree. The wolves clawed through the web, and sped toward Spider Crusader. Spider Crusader backflipped, and shot some webs at the wolves. The webs attached to the wolves. Spider Crusader pulled on the web, and threw the wolves in to the building. Spider Crusader sped in to the wolves, and picked them up in to the air. Spider Crusader smashed the wolves in to the ground, and stabbed his web knife in to their necks. The wolves laid on the ground in puddles of blood. Spider Crusader and Justin walked out of the courtyard of Oasis Falls High School. Spider Crusader and

Justin walked down the street. Police cars were speeding through the street, and the citizens were walking through the sidewalks. An crane malfunctioned, and swung its wrecking ball through a building. The building debris were falling on top of the citizens. Justin sprung in to action, and tackled the citizens in to the back alley. Spider Crusader shot webs at the falling debris. The webs attached to the sides of the building, and wrapped around the falling debris. Spider Crusader back-flipped in to the air, and ran on the side of the building. Spider Crusader used his webs as a slingshot, and slingshot himself on to the wrecking ball. Spider Crusader crawled on the wrecking ball, and hung on to the crane. Spider Crusader hung on to the crane, and crawled toward the control panel. Spider Crusader pulled open the control panel with his arms. Spider Crusader disabled the crane by pulling out the electrical wires, that were in the control panel. The crane lost its balance, and starting falling on to the ground. Spider Crusader wrapped up the crane with his webs, to slow down the speed of the crane. The crane fell on to the ground. Spider Crusader hung upside down from his web, and landed on the ground. The citizens cheered for Spider Crusader, as Justin walked out of the back alley. Spider Crusader refilled his web shooters, as he walked toward Justin. Justin and Spider Crusader walked further down the street. Justin and Spider Crusader walked to a hot dog stand, and bought some hot dogs. Justin and Spider Crusader sat on the bench, that was next to the hog dog stand. Justin ate his hot dog. Spider Crusader detracted his helmet, and ate his hot dog. Spider Crusader retracted his helmet, and relaxed on the bench. The birds were tweeting in the background. Justin relaxed on the bench, and listened to the birds. Justin and Spider Crusader wrapped their arms around each other. Justin and Spider Crusader hugged each other. The wind blew through Justin's hair. The tree blew in the wind. Police cars sped through the area, and they were patrolling the streets. The sun disappeared in the sky, and the moon rise. The sky was clear, and the stars were shining. An group of squirrels crawled up to the bench, where Justin and Spider Crusader were sitting. The squirrels crawled up the bench, and jumped on to Justin's hair. The squirrels chewed on Justin's hair. Justin whacked the squirrels out of his hair. The squirrels fell on to the ground, and rubbed their heads. The squirrels crawled up Justin's leg. Justin lit his leg on fire with his flames, and the squirrels burnt to a crisp. Police cars were speeding through the area, with their sirens on. Thieves were speeding away from the police cars, and shooting at the police cars with their weapons. Spider Crusader's spider sense was tingling, and he sprung in to action. Spider Crusader backflipped off of the bench, and detracted his helmet. Spider Crusader's helmet covered his face, as he swung in to the air with his webs. Spider Crusader shot a web at the car of the thieves. The web attached to the car's hood. Spider Crusader grabbed the web, and slingshot himself on to the car. Spider Crusader landed on the car, and punched the windshield with his arm. The windshield shattered to pieces, as the thieves lost control of the car. The car spun out of control, and smashed through the streets. Spider Crusader hung on to the car, and crawled on to the side door. Spider Crusader shot a web at the window, and pulled it off of the car. Spider Crusader crawled in to the car, and stabbed his web knife in to the thieves. The thieves laid on the floor of the car in puddles of blood. Spider Crusader kicked the door open with his leg, and climbed out of it. Spider Crusader crawled on to the hood of the car, and shot webs at the tires. The webs attached to the tires. Spider Crusader backflipped off of the car, and wrapped the car with some webs. The webs wrapped around the car. Spider Crusader pulled on the webs, and lifted the car in to the air. Spider Crusader shot a web at the car, while it was in the air. The web attached the car, to the side of the building. Spider Crusader shot a web, and hung backwards. Spider Crusader landed on the ground, as the citizens saw the chaos from the car. Spider Crusader swung through the air, and landed next to the bench. Spider Crusader sat next to Justin, as he retracted his helmet. Spider Crusader relaxed on the bench. At the villain hideout, Otto was cleaning the hideout with a dust pan. He noticed an folder on the shelf. Otto picked up the folder, and read through it. The folder was filled with experiment research about various species, such as vultures and other animals. Otto found the research fascinating and was amazed at all of the information that he found. Otto smiled, as he put the dust pan away. Otto walked to the computer, and logged in to it. Otto tapped on some keys, and loaded up the data for the research. Otto clicked on the research, and loaded it on to the computer. Otto was amazed by all of the data. Otto scrolled through the data, and wrote some stuff down on his notepad. Otto drew concept art of vulture wings on his notepad. Otto tapped some buttons on the computer, and put his notepad in to the scanner. The drawing of the concept art got scanned in to the computer, and the machines started manufacturing the vulture wings, in front of Otto. The machines finished manufacturing the vulture wings. In the background, there was a sound of the hideout doors opening. Drew walked through the villain hideout! Drew walked in to the laboratory. Otto got up from the computer, and walked toward Drew. Otto walked to Drew, and guided him to the machine. Otto opened up the machine. Drew walked in to the machine. Drew laid in the machine. Otto connected the wires to Drew's body, and closed the machine. Otto walked to the computer, and sat in the chair. Otto tapped some buttons on the computer, and loaded the vulture DNA in to Drew's body. Otto tapped the buttons, and dragged some files on the screen. Otto combined the vulture DNA with Supersonic Warrior's DNA. Otto loaded the merged DNA in to Drew's body. The computer beeped, as it finished the process. Otto logged off the computer, and got up from his chair. Otto walked to the machine, and opened it up. Otto disconnected the wires from Drew's body. Drew opened his eyes, and walked out of the machine. Drew and Otto walked to the vulture wings. Drew attached the vulture wings to his body. The vulture wings activated, and attached themselves to Drew's back. Drew jumped in the air, and flew around the area. The training bots shot their weapons at Drew. Drew dodged the blaster bolts, and flew toward the training bots. Drew swung his wings at the training bots, and smashed them to pieces. Otto was amazed at Drew's strength. Drew jumped on the walls, and landed on the ground. Otto summoned more training bots. The training bots shot their weapons at Drew. Drew flew towards the training bots, and grabbed one of them with his legs. Drew threw the training bot at the table. The training bot smashed through the glass containers, and exploded. Otto cleaned up the glass shards, while Drew flew toward the other training bot. Drew smashed the other training bot in to the wall. The other training bot exploded, as Drew landed on the ground. Otto was amazed by Drew's skills. Drew sat on the bench, and drank a bottle of water. Drew threw the bottle of water in to the recycling bin. Drew got up from the bench, and smashed the window with his wing. Drew jumped out of the window, and flew in to the air. Drew was flying through the air, and heard the cars speeding through the streets. The city was bustling in action, as the citizens of Zoomopolis were living their lives. There were a group of citizens, buying ice cream from the ice cream truck. Drew flew toward the ice cream stand, and landed on top of it. The citizens were terrified in fear! Drew swung his wings at the citizens, and killed them. The citizens laid on the ground, in puddles of blood. The ice cream stand manager grabbed some ice cream bars from his stand, and threw them at Drew. Drew flew in to the air, and dodged the ice cream bars. Drew flew toward the ice cream stand manager, and grabbed him with his legs. Drew flew in to the air, as the ice cream stand manager struggled in his grip. Drew flew toward one of the buildings, and smashed through the glass windows. The glass shards from the glass windows hit the ice cream stand manager, as Drew flew in the air. Drew flew toward the sky, and spun in the air. Drew flew toward the skyscraper! Drew flew over the skyscraper, and dropped the ice cream stand manager. The ice cream stand manager fell from Drew's grip, and smashed through the skyscraper. The skyscraper crumbled to pieces on top of the ice cream stand manager, as he smashed in to the ground. The ice cream stand manager laid on the ground, in a puddle of blood. The citizens were horrified at the destruction of the skyscraper. The police officers saw the destruction, and cleaned up the debris. Drew flew back to the villain hideout. Drew flew through the window of the villain hideout, and landed next to Otto. Otto was watching the security footage on the computer, and was amazed by all of the destruction. An security alert from Otto's hero tracker went off on Otto's computer. Otto opened up the security alert! An map of Zoomopolis showed up on Otto's screen. The map showed the location of Spider Crusader's secret hideout. Otto and Drew smiled at the discovery. Otto said, "It's time to pay our favorite little spider and his buddy a small visit!" Drew smiled and said, "Sounds good, boss, I will cause them pain and misery!" Drew jumped in to the air, and flew out of the window with his vulture wings. Drew flew towards Spider Crusader's secret hideout. Down the street, Justin and Spider Crusader were in Spider Crusader's secret hideout. Spider Crusader's secret hideout was filled with gadgets, and other essential items to stay alive. Spider Crusader and Justin walked in to Spider Crusader's laboratory. The laboratory was filled with books, machines, and gadgets. Justin was amazed by all of the gadgets, that he can use to defeat super villains. Spider Crusader walked toward the desk, and upgraded his webshooters. Justin laid on the bed in the laboratory. Spider Crusader shot a web at the ceiling, and hung upside down on it. Spider Crusader cleaned the dust off of the shelves in the laboratory. Spider Crusader backflipped on to the ground. Justin got up from the bed in the laboratory, and walked in to the bathroom. Justin took off his clothes, and walked in to the shower. Justin turned on the water, and washed the dirt out of his hair. Justin washed the dirt off of his body. Justin turned off the shower, and walked out of it. Justin dried himself off, and put his clothes back on. Justin walked out of the bathroom. Spider Crusader was sitting in the chair, and reading the news on the computer. In the background, cars were speeding down the street, next to the hideout. Justin laid on the bed. Justin closed his eyes! The moon shined through the windows of Spider Crusader's secret hideout. Spider Crusader activated the cleaning robot. The cleaning robot went around the laboratory, and vacuumed the dust from the floors. The cleaning robot washed the floors, and reorganized the shelves. The cleaning robot finished cleaning the secret hideout. The walls of the secret hideout shook, as Drew landed on the side of the window. Drew punched the window with his fist, and shattered it to pieces. Drew flew through the smashed window, and grabbed the cleaning robot with his feet. Drew threw the cleaning robot in to the wall. The cleaning robot smashed in to the wall, and exploded. Spider Crusader grabbed his web shooters off of the laboratory desk, and attached them to his wrist. Drew walked through the laboratory toward Spider Crusader. Spider Crusader shot a web at Drew. Drew sliced the web to shreds with his vulture wings. Drew sped toward Spider Crusader, and tackled him in to the wall. Spider Crusader growled, and backflipped over Drew. Spider Crusader kicked Drew in the back. Drew smashed in to the wall, and growled. Drew flew in to the air, and flew towards Spider Crusader. Drew hovered over Spider Crusader, and wrapped his legs around Spider Crusader's body. Justin woke up, and got up from the bed. Justin saw Drew and said, "Let Him Go!" Drew laughed and said, "Over my dead body, little shrimp!" Justin threw a fire ball at Drew. Drew dodged the fire ball, and flew out of the window. Justin ran after Drew, and backflipped out of the window. Justin summoned a sheet of flames, and followed Drew. Drew flew in to the sky, and smashed through several buildings. The glass shattered around Drew and Spider Crusader, as the buildings fell on to the streets, and killed multiple citizens of Zoomopolis. Drew flew towards the villain hideout. Drew flew in to the villain hideout, and landed next to the experiment machine. Drew opened the experiment machine, and threw Spider Crusader in to it. Drew attached the wires to Spider Crusader's body, and closed the machine. Otto walked in to the room, and was pleased at Drew's success. Drew logged on to the computer, and started up the machine. The machine spun its gears and the wires electrocuted Spider Crusader. Spider Crusader screamed in pain, as his blood flowed through the wires, that are attached to his body. Spider Crusader's blood poured in to a tube, that the machine was attached to. The tube was filled to the top with Spider crusader's blood. Otto walked to the tube, and detached it from the machine. Otto sealed the tube, and put it on to the analyze pad. The analyze pad was connected to the computer. The machine went idle, and the electricity stopped flowing through the wires. Spider Crusader laid in the machine, and was catching his breath. Otto and Drew analyzed Spider Crusader's blood, and was amazed by his DNA. Otto and Drew saved the data to their database. A fireball flew through the window, and hit Otto in the face! Otto smashed in to the wall, and laid on the ground. Justin back-flipped through the window, and tackled Drew in to the ground. Justin growled, as his eyes glowed red. Justin shot a fire laser from his eyes at Drew. Drew blocked the fire laser with his vulture wings, and hit Justin in the chest. Justin slid backwards. Drew roundhouse kicked Justin in the face. Justin rolled on the ground. Justin got up from the ground. Drew flew in to Justin, and hit him in the chest with his vulture wings. Justin slid backwards! Drew used his voice modulation and used his vocal blast on Justin. Justin smashed in to the wall, and laid on the ground. Drew walked toward Justin, and smiled! Drew said, "The slippery hero has fallen!" Justin growled and said, "Don't count me out yet!" Norman walked in to the room and smiled at the success of his team mates. Drew stepped on Justin's chest and said, "You might want to change your tone, hero!" Norman clapped and said, "I am proud of both of you for capturing the heroes!" Norman said, "Drew, put the little pest in to the other machine! Let's have some fun, and torture them!" Drew grabbed Justin by his neck, and picked him up from the ground. Drew lifted Justin in to the air, and opened the other machine ! Drew put Justin in to the other machine, and connected the wires to his body!. Drew closed up the other machine, and walked to the computer. Drew activated the other machine. The machine spun to life, as the electricity flowed through the wires. Drew set the electricity values on the machines, and sent the electrical energy through the wires. The electricity in the wires electrocuted Justin and Spider Crusader, as they screamed in pain. The villains laughed manically, as the heroes were getting tortured by the machines. Spider Crusader and Justin's blood mixed together, as it poured in to the tube on the desk. The tube filled to the top with the blood! Norman disconnected the tube from the computer, and attached the tube to the needle. Norman injected the needle to his arm. Norman's body grew in muscle mass and strength, as the blood flowed through his body. Norman's eyes glowed green, as he smiled. Justin growled, as his eyes glowed red. Justin's body ignited an blast of flames. Everything in the lab exploded, as Justin landed on the ground. Spider Crusader hid behind the shelf! Justin sped in to Otto, and grabbed him by his neck. Justin lifted Otto in to the air, and set Otto's body on fire with his flames. Otto's body burnt in to ashes! Drew growled, and hit Justin in the chest with his vulture wings. Justin summoned an aura of flames! The aura of flames burnt Drew's vulture wings to a crisp. Drew was terrified in fear! Justin punched Drew in the face with a fire blast. Drew smashed in to the wall, and laid next to it. Justin sped in to Drew, and grabbed him by the neck. Justin lifted Drew in to the air, and smashed him in to the ground. Justin held Drew on to the ground, and punched him in the face, multiple times. Justin set his hand on Drew's chest, and set his body on fire. Drew's body turned to ash! Justin got up from the ground, and wiped the dust off of his body. Norman growled, as his eyes glowed green. Norman sped in to Justin, and punched him in the face. Justin slid backwards! Norman walked closer to Justin, as he smiled! Justin shot fire blasts at Norman. The fire blasts fizzled, as they bounced off of Norman's body! Norman said, "That tickled, time for me to smash some sense in to you!" Norman grabbed Justin by his neck, and smashed him through the table. Justin laid on the ground! Norman held Justin on the ground, and grabbed a glass container off of the desk! Norman smashed the glass container on top of Justin's head! The glass container broke, as blood leaked from Justin's head! Norman punched Justin in the face, multiple times, as he laid on the ground. Justin ignited a fire blast from his body. Norman slid backwards, as Justin got up from the ground. Norman grabbed a couple of fire bombs from the desk, and threw them at Justin. The fire bombs exploded, and the explosion smashed Justin in to the wall. Justin laid against the wall, and rubbed his head. Norman sped in to Justin, and grabbed his neck. Norman smashed Justin in to the ground. Justin laid on the ground! Norman ignited a blast from his body. The blast covered the area, and exploded everything in the villain hideout, and set everything on fire. Norman jumped on to the glider, that was sitting in the villain hideout. Norman flew out of the villain hideout, and patrolled the city. The debris from the explosion fell on top of Justin, and buried him. Spider Crusader got up from his hiding spot, and web slinged himself to the debris. The villain hideout was falling apart around him, with the flames growing bigger. Spider Crusader lifted the debris off of Justin. Spider Crusader picked up Justin's body! Spider Crusader laid Justin on his back, and web swung around the villain hideout. The villain hideout was collapsing on itself. Spider Crusader shot a web at the window, and pulled on the web. The web shattered the window. Spider Crusader web swung through the window, and landed on the ground. Spider Crusader walked to the bench! Spider Crusader laid Justin on the bench. Spider Crusader laid his hand on Justin's chest. The health indicator on Spider Crusader's wrist showed that Justin had a pulse, but he is barely breathing. Spider Crusader picked up Justin's body, and laid him on his back. Spider Crusader web swung in to the air, and swung through the city. Spider Crusader saw the courtyard for Oasis Falls High School. Spider Crusader landed in front of Oasis Falls High School, and opened up the doors with his webs. Spider Crusader walked through the hallway, and analyzed everything around him. Spider Crusader found the science lab, and walked toward it. Spider Crusader walked in to the science lab, and opened up the healing tube. Spider Crusader laid Justin in to the healing tube, and connected the wires to his body. Spider Crusader closed the healing tube. Spider Crusader walked to the chair, and sat in it. Spider Crusader logged in to the computer, that was sitting on the desk. Spider Crusader pressed some buttons on the computer, and the healing machine activated. The healing energy flowed through the wires in to Justin's body.

Josh Zimmer is an crazy individual with an extreme imagination. He loves to have fun by listening to music, writing stories, and playing video games of various genres such as platforming, multiplayer online games, role playing games, and sports games. His favorite technology brands are Nintendo and Microsoft. They are wonderful role models for the industry. He commands an army of cats to his will with hugs, love, and snacks. He makes the cats purr and meow with happiness.

www.ingramcontent.com/pod-product-compliance
Lightning Source LLC
Chambersburg PA
CBHW071015120726
47910CB00004B/1535